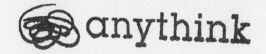 anythink

D0460642

Kitten
and the
the Night
Watchman

For Beebe and all the strays
—J. S.

For Seunghan and Jiyoon, with much love
—T. Y.

SIMON & SCHUSTER BOOKS FOR YOUNG READERS
An imprint of Simon & Schuster Children's Publishing Division
1230 Avenue of the Americas, New York, New York 10020
Text copyright © 2007, 2018 by John Sullivan
Illustrations copyright © 2018 by Taeeun Yoo
SIMON & SCHUSTER BOOKS FOR YOUNG READERS is a trademark of Simon & Schuster, Inc.
For information about special discounts for bulk purchases,
please contact Simon & Schuster Special Sales at 1-866-506-1949 or business@simonandschuster.com.
The Simon & Schuster Speakers Bureau can bring authors to your live event. For more information or to book an event,
contact the Simon & Schuster Speakers Bureau at 1-866-248-3049 or visit our website at www.simonspeakers.com.
Book design by Laurent Linn
The text for this book was set in Providence Sans.
The illustrations for this book were created using digital and hand-printed textures.
Manufactured in China
0718 SCP
First Edition
2 4 6 8 10 9 7 5 3 1
CIP data for this book is available from the Library of Congress.
ISBN 978-1-4814-6191-7
ISBN 978-1-4814-6192-4 (eBook)

Kitten
and
the
Night
Watchman

WRITTEN BY John Sullivan

ILLUSTRATED BY Taeeun Yoo

A Paula Wiseman Book

SIMON & SCHUSTER BOOKS FOR YOUNG READERS

New York London Toronto Sydney New Delhi

The night watchman hugs
his wife and children . . .

and drives to work.

Every hour he makes his rounds, alone.

He checks the doors.

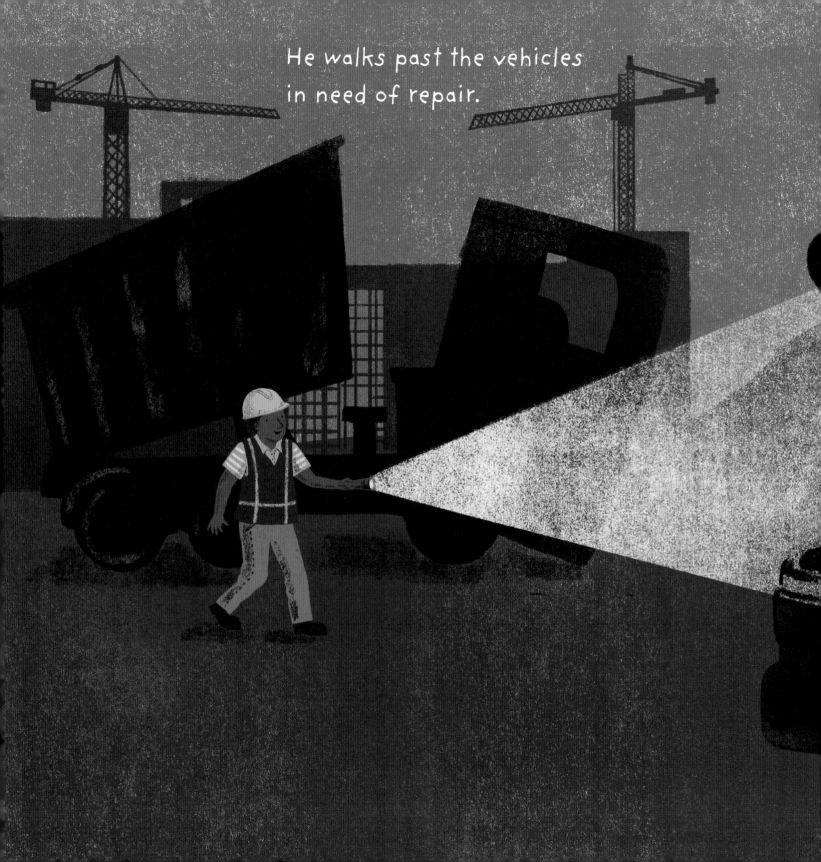

He walks past the vehicles in need of repair.

ki-DEE

ki-DEE

ki-DEE

He surprises a killdeer.

Stars twinkle. The full moon
shines like an old friend.

He thinks of his boy and girl,
safe and asleep at home.

"Back again?" he asks.

Garbage trucks line up
like circus elephants.

An excavator bows
like a strange giraffe.

A backhoe rises
like a giant insect.

EEEEEERRRRROOOOOOOOOOMMMMMM

And all is quiet again.

The night watchman feeds the
kitten from his own dinner and
settles back into the chair.

The kitten tickles his nose
with her whiskers.

Each time the night watchman makes another round, the kitten follows.

A crane fly looks like a huge mosquito. A beetle bumps against the yard light.

peent

peent

peent

A nighthawk calls out.

The night watchman holds the door open.

The kitten isn't there.
She is nowhere to be seen.

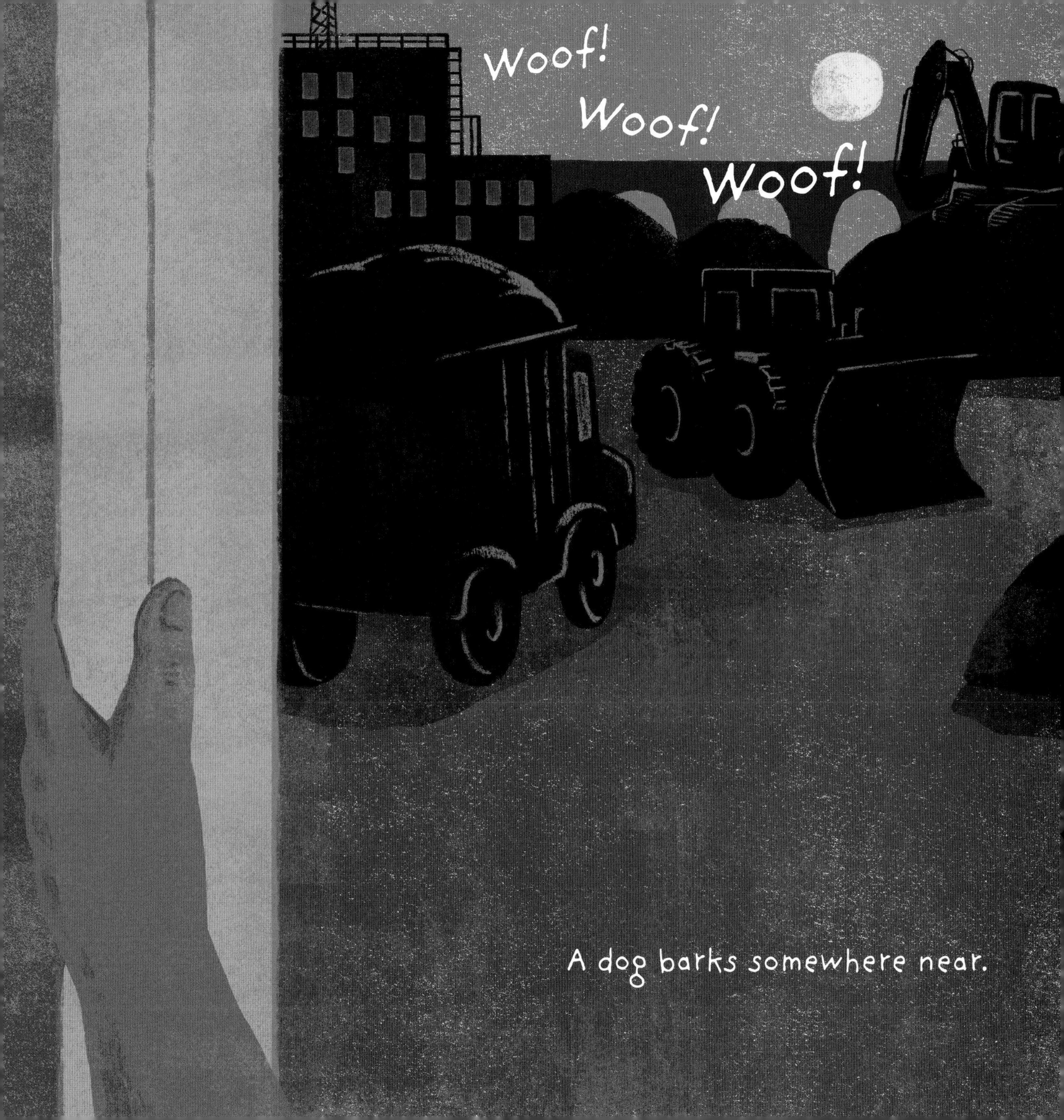

A dog barks somewhere near.

A car races down a street.

RRRRRRRRRRROOOOOOOAAAAAARRRRRRRRRRRRR

A rumble-*clack*-*clack*.

A freight train passes by.

The night watchman sits at his desk.
He is too worried to read.

He catches a moth. It's soft and gentle.
He carries it outside.

"Where have you been, kitty?"

The moon travels across the sky.

The hour hand circles the clock.

The night watchman and the kitten
work through the night.

Bird songs sprinkle the air.

It's time for the night
watchman to drive home.
But this time he is not alone.

"Come along, kitty. I know a boy and girl who will want to give you a name."